Cover Design and illustration by Zuzana Svobodová
Book design by Peggy Collins, Bookery Design Shop
Author's photograph by Aliyah Dastour

ISBNs:
978-0-9985362-6-2 (Softcover)
978-0-9985362-7-9 (Hardcover)
978-0-9985362-8-6 (Ebook)

Library of Congress Control Number: 2018953054

Summary: Zetta was once a lonely poinsettia sitting on a box with the rest of the stock at the Miller Plant and Seed. It was the beginning of the holiday season – so there was a reason To Be. Then one day the season went away, but Zetta discovers she still has reason "To Be."

JUV057000   JUVENILE FICTION / Stories in Verse
JUV017010   JUVENILE FICTION / Holidays & Celebrations / Christmas & Advent
JUV039140   JUVENILE FICTION / Social Themes / Self-Esteem & Self-Reliance
JUV039050 JUVENILE FICTION / Social Themes / Emotions & Feelings

Printed and bound in the United States of America
First Edition

ZETTA THE POINSETTIA

WRITTEN BY ALMA HAMMOND   ILLUSTRATED BY ZUZANA SVOBODOVÁ

THIS BOOK
BELONGS TO:

SWEETBEET
BOOKS

FOR YOU.

/POIN·SET·TI·A/

A small Mexican plant with large, red, modified leaves surrounding small yellow buds or flowers. It is popular as a houseplant at Christmas.

SWEETBEET BOOKS

ZETTA THE POINSETTIA

BY ALMA HAMMOND

ILLUSTRATED BY ZUZANA SVOBODOVÁ

Zetta was once a lonely Poinsettia
perched upon a box
with the rest of the stock
at the Miller Plant and Seed.

It was the beginning of the holiday season.

Surely there was a reason
TO BE.

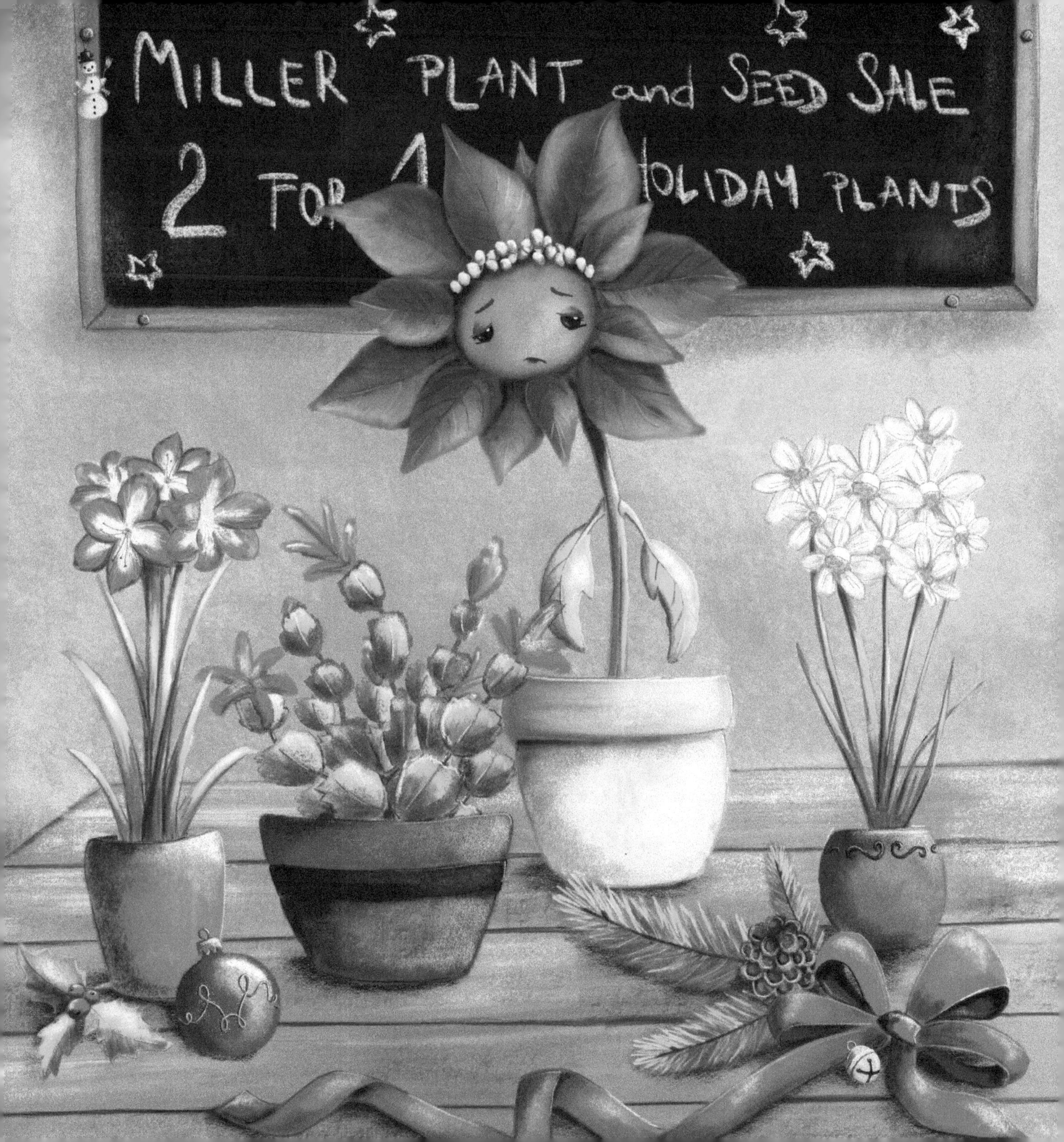
MILLER PLANT and SEED SALE

After what seemed like a long while,
Zetta begged with a smile,

"OH, WON'T SOMEONE PLEASE TAKE ME?"

Soon a little girl with
wide eyes caught sight,
of the bright red vision,
off to the right.

"Oh, we need one of these!"
said the girl, with a sneeze. A tug at
Mom's coat brought Zetta afloat
into the family's empty shopping tote.

AAA CHOOOO

Then to the car, and then to their home,
where Zetta was placed on her throne—
the mantel—in the center
of the other holiday trimmings.

Awwwwwwwwwwww

With each day that passed,
Zetta let out a cheery gasp that
could only be matched by the joyful
sounds of the holiday season:

GIFT
WRAP
CRACKLING

FIRES
A 'SNAPPING

AND HOLIDAY
SLIPPERS
TIPPY-TAPPING

Then one day,
the excitement went away.

Boxes and wrap
thrown out in a snap.

Fire pits forgotten,
floral arrangements
gone rotten.

All the fuzzy slippers and
decorations carefully stored,
and the dead tree dragged
out the back door.

But there remained Zetta—
Zetta, the Poinsettia.

Still alive and strong
from the care
and the love.

"But what of me?

What now
is my reason
TO BE?

Will I go the way of the Tree?"

Zetta shivered, as Mom took her down from her throne.

Placing her by the light of a window,
she was no longer alone.

Zetta once again became warm,

and grew, and thrived.

When spring came,
Zetta was replanted
in a bigger pot and
brought outside
where the light could
reach her even better.

Now flanked by the front door,
growing more and more,

Zetta knew now that whether
or not holidays were in sight,

she would always
reach toward the light,

for she still had reason
TO BE—
to brighten the lives of others!

FUN FACTS ABOUT THE POINSETTIA

ONE

The flower part of the poinsettia is the yellow,
clustered buds in the center, not the red part of the plant.
The red part is actually modified leaves.

TWO

Red is the most popular color of poinsettia, however, the plant also comes in salmon,
apricot, yellow, cream, and white, and colors in-between.
There are also speckled or marbled types. A new type comes out each year!

THREE

People buy over 34 million poinsettias each year. Poinsettias are the top-selling potted plant!

FOUR

California grows the most poinsettias, followed by North Carolina and Texas.

FIVE

Dr. Joel Roberts Poinsett, the first U.S. Ambassador to Mexico,
introduced the plant to the U.S. in 1828.

SIX

December 12 is National Poinsettia Day, observed since the mid-1800s.

SEVEN

Despite what many people think, the poinsettia is rarely poisonous.
That said, it is not edible, could make you or your pets sick, and should not be eaten!
Besides, they don't taste very good anyway!

ALMA HAMMOND is the award winning author of two picture books in her "Travel with Me" series, "Super Rooster and Wonder Cat," set in Tahiti; and "Andre the Five-Star Cat," set in Paris, France. Zetta the Poinsettia is her third book and inspired by the decision to keep a poinsettia plant after the holidays. Alma lives with her husband Bob, dog Stazi, and two cats, Violet, and Daisy, in Bethesda, MD. When she isn't writing, Alma enjoys yoga, cooking, and traveling.

ZUZANA SVOBODOVÁ

Illustrator Zuzana Svobodová uses both digital and traditional techniques, as well as the world of fantasy delivered happily by her own children to bring stories to life. Zuzana lives with her husband Roman, and two children Lucia and Jakub, in Slovakia. When she isn't working on illustrations, she enjoys drawing, teaching yoga, coffee, dreaming, and baking sweets.

CPSIA information can be obtained
at www.ICGtesting.com
Printed in the USA
LVHW072015200723
752770LV00004B/153